CONTENTS

ERRO

PLATEAU OF LENG

PHANTOM FOREST

POISON SEA

VULCAN MOUNTAINS

LAKE OF GOLD

METAL MOON

DIAMOND MINES

MONSTER ZOO

PITS OF NO RETURN

PRISON STRONGHOLDS

SWAMP OF FLAME

SCARLET JUNGLE

PRISON ENERGY DRIVES

SPACE PORT PRISONER INTAKE

ABYSS OF GIANTS

ZAK

THE PRISONERS

ZAK NINE

Zak is a teenage boy from Earth Base Zeta. He dreams of piloting a star fighter one day. Zak is very brave and is a quick thinker. But his enthusiasm often leads him into trouble.

ERRO

Erro is a teenage furling from the planet Quom. He has the fur, long tail, sharp eyes and claws of his species. Erro is often impatient with Zak's reckless ways. But he shares his friend's love of adventure.

THE PRISON PLANET

Alcatraz . . . there is no escape from this terrifying prison planet. It's filled with dungeons, traps, endless deserts and other dangers. Zak Nine and his alien friend, Erro, are trapped here. They had sneaked onto a ship hoping to see an awesome space battle. But the ship landed on Alcatraz instead. Now they have to work together if they ever hope to escape!

ZAK'S STORY . . . HIDDEN DANGERS >>>

My friend Erro and I were lucky to escape from the Maze of Thorns – and its nest of giant vampire beetles! Now we're walking next to a strange golden lake. Erro has spotted an ancient building nearby. We're going to check it out and see if it's safe to hide inside . . . >>>>

CHAPTER ONE: GOLDEN MYSTERY

It's almost night.

Erro and I are sneaking around a large lake. The tall reeds growing next to the lake hide us well.

But there's something weird about this place. The lake seems to be filled with liquid gold.

"Where does the gold come from?" I ask.

"Maybe from there," says Erro, pointing to something nearby.

On the edge of the lake sits a huge golden building. The walls are crumbling. Its windows are covered with rusty bars.

We arrive at the building and carefully enter. Inside, the building is silent and very creepy.

"I think this was an old prison," I say.

We step into a large, empty space. The wide floor is covered with gold and black squares.

This looks like a big draughts board, I think.

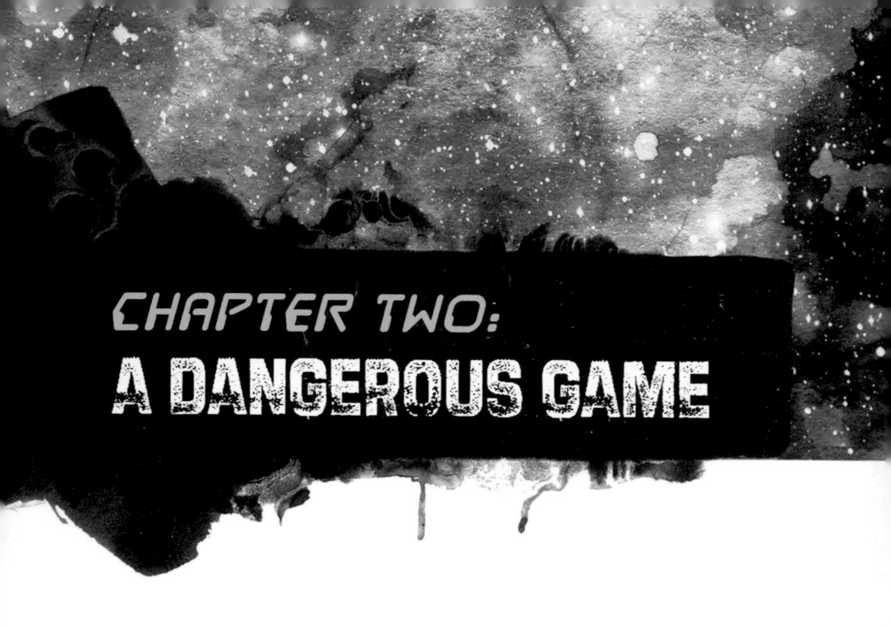

CHAPTER TWO: A DANGEROUS GAME

"I'll play the black squares," I say.

I start hopping from one to another. Erro just stares at me.

"It's an old Earth game," I tell him. "I'll tell you the rules as we go along. You play on the gold squares."

"All right," Erro says, then steps onto a gold square.

FFFWWWIISSSSSHH!!

The gold square suddenly slides open, and Erro drops through the floor!

"Erro!" I call out, as I race towards him.

But a black square suddenly opens beneath me like a trapdoor. We both fall down into a long, dark tunnel.

"Ouch!"

I land in the middle of a golden table next to Erro. There are eight golden plates on the table. It looks as if it has been set for dinner.

"Where are we?" I ask.

We look around the dark stone room. Above us, the ceiling and the trapdoors are lost in darkness.

CHAPTER THREE: THE OCTAGON

The table has eight sides. Each side faces a different wall. The room is shaped like an octagon. Each of the walls has a golden door.

"One of those doors should lead out of here," I say.

But which one? I wonder as I climb off the table.

I walk up to the closest door and pull it open.

I start to step through, but Erro shouts.

"Be careful!" he says. "We don't know what this place is."

I turn back to face my friend. "I think this is a feast room and–"

KKRUNNNNCH!!

Just inside the door, two stone walls have smashed together. Then the door swings shut.

That was close . . . too close. I was almost a human pancake!

H7

"This whole place is a trap," says Erro with wide eyes.

"Maybe this is where they locked up special prisoners," I say.

"And where they died," my Quom friend says fearfully.

I look at the other seven doors.

"We still have to get out of here," I say. "I'll be more careful next time."

I slowly open the next door.

CHAPTER FOUR: MORE TRAPS

The passage inside the door is completely black. I look back at the table where Erro is sitting.

"Hand me one of those plates," I say.

Erro pulls at a plate. "It is stuck to the table."

"All of them?" I ask.

He tries all the plates and finds one that's loose.

I put the plate on its edge and give it a push. It rolls through the door and into the darkness.

There's no sound.

Erro steps up to the door. "This one must be safe," he says.

But then we hear a sliding sound. We stand by the door and listen carefully.

splish!

Far away, the plate has fallen into some water.

“These doors are all dangerous!” shouts Erro.

“But we can’t stay here,” I say. “We’ll starve to death.”

“Too bad those plates don’t have any food,” says Erro. “I am starving.”

I look at the feast table.

"Why was only one plate loose?" I ask.

"I do not know," says Erro.

Frustrated, Erro pulls open another door. The door just opens to a wall. There is no passage.

"Nothing too dangerous there," I say.

KKRRRKKGGRR!

Suddenly a grinding sound comes from above us.

I look up. I can see the ceiling now. It's no longer hidden in darkness.

That's because it's moving closer – to crush us!

CHAPTER FIVE: THE DOOR PLATE

"We'll be smashed!" I shout.

"Try all the doors!" Erro shouts back.

But by now, the moving ceiling has reached the doors.

"No use. We cannot pull them open," he says. "The ceiling is in the way!"

He's right. The stone ceiling is blocking the doors from opening.

I look back at the table. We can't hide under it. It is slowly sliding into the floor – plates and all.

Soon the ceiling is forcing us to our hands and knees. Then I realize something.

"Wait! That loose plate!" I yell. "Where did you get it?"

Erro points to the far side of the table. I quickly crawl to the door on that side.

This door doesn't pull open either. *It pushes out!*

"The loose plate was a clue!" I shout.

Erro and I crawl through the doorway as fast as we can.

"That whole room was like a big game," I say. "A dangerous one."

"I am glad you are good at games," whispers Erro.

"Me too," I reply. "But let's hope I'm also good at finding a way out of this place. Let's go."

GLOSSARY

ancient from a long time ago

dungeon strong, dark prison or cell, usually underground

frustrated angry or upset about something

octagon shape or space with eight sides

passage corridor or tunnel

reeds tall grass with long, narrow leaves and joined stems that often grows in wetlands

species group of living things that share similar features

trapdoor door often hidden or disguised in a floor that slides or swings open

TALK ABOUT IT

1. When the boys enter the golden building, they find what looks like a huge draughts board on the floor. Do you think Zak was wise to try to play a game on it? What would you have done if you were in Zak's place?

2. The mysterious building and everything in it seems to be made of gold. Why do you think this is? Why do you think a prison planet would have a golden building next to a lake?

3. The boys barely escape being crushed by the strange room's stone ceiling. Why do you think the room had just one door that could open to let someone escape? Explain your answer.

WRITE ABOUT IT

1. At the beginning of the story, Zak mentions that he and Erro escaped the Maze of Thorns and a nest of giant vampire beetles. Write your own Zak and Erro adventure describing how they escaped.

2. Zak and Erro open only four doors in the strange room. What do you think were behind the other doors? Use your imagination and write a list of dangerous traps hidden behind them.

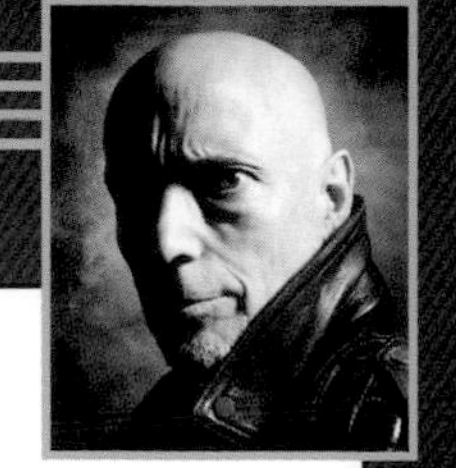

ABOUT THE AUTHOR

Michael Dahl is the author of more than 300 books for young readers, including the Library of Doom series. He is a huge fan of Star Trek, Star Wars and Doctor Who. He has a fear of closed-in spaces, but has visited several prisons, dungeons and strongholds, both ancient and modern. He made a daring escape from each one. Luckily, the guards still haven't found him.

ABOUT THE ILLUSTRATOR

Patricio Clarey was born in 1978 in Argentina. He graduated in fine arts at the School of Visual Arts Martín Malharro, specializing in illustration and graphic design. Patricio currently lives in Barcelona, Spain, where he works as a freelance graphic designer and illustrator. He has created several comics and graphic novels, and his work has been featured in several books and other publications.